THE VISCOUNT'S TEMPTING MINX

DUKES OF WAR #1

ERICA RIDLEY

Original Title: *The Viscount's Christmas Temptation*

This is a work of fiction. Names, characters, places, and incidents are the product of the author's imagination or are used fictitiously. Any resemblance to actual events, locales, or persons, living or dead, is purely coincidental.

Cover design © Teresa Spreckelmeyer

Model photography: VJ Dunraven, PeriodImages

ALSO BY ERICA RIDLEY

The *Dukes of War*:

The Viscount's Tempting Minx

The Earl's Defiant Wallflower

The Captain's Bluestocking Mistress

The Major's Faux Fiancée

The Brigadier's Runaway Bride

The Pirate's Tempting Stowaway

The Duke's Accidental Wife

***Rogues to Riches*:**

Lord of Chance

Lord of Pleasure

Lord of Night

Lord of Temptation

Lord of Secrets

Lord of Vice

The *12 Dukes of Christmas*:

Once Upon a Duke

Kiss of a Duke

Wish Upon a Duke

Never Say Duke

Dukes, Actually

The Duke's Bride

The Duke's Embrace

The Duke's Desire

Dawn With a Duke

One Night With a Duke

Ten Days With a Duke

Forever Your Duke

***Gothic Love Stories*:**

Too Wicked to Kiss

Too Sinful to Deny

Too Tempting to Resist

Too Wanton to Wed

***Magic & Mayhem*:**

Kissed by Magic

Must Love Magic

Smitten by Magic

The *Wicked Dukes Club*:

One Night for Seduction by Erica Ridley

One Night of Surrender by Darcy Burke

One Night of Passion by Erica Ridley

One Night of Scandal by Darcy Burke

One Night to Remember by Erica Ridley

One Night of Temptation by Darcy Burke

ACKNOWLEDGMENTS

As always, I could not have written this book without the invaluable support of my critique partners. Huge thanks go out to Emma Locke and Erica Monroe for their advice, encouragement, and slaps upside the head. You are the best!

I also want to thank the *Dukes of War* facebook group, the Historical Romance Book Club, and my fabulous street team. Your enthusiasm makes the romance happen. Thank you so much!

Four left for war...
One stayed home.

CHAPTER 1

December 12, 1815
London, England

Lady Amelia Pembroke glanced up from the well-worn almanac in her lap as her brother, the Duke of Ravenwood, strode into the yellow parlor with a distracted frown.

The yellow parlor, despite being part and parcel of the winter ducal mansion, was strictly Amelia's domain. The bookcases were lined with rows of leather-bound journals containing page after page written in Amelia's small, precise hand. The cherrywood table nearest the bay windows contained the day's correspondence, stacked according to priority. The oversized basket beside her wingback chair brimmed with a week's worth of periodicals, the ink worn gray from having been handled many times.

Amelia marked her place with a crisp green ribbon and set the almanac aside. Her brother's presence could only mean he needed her wisdom on some matter. There was nothing she cherished more than the opportunity to put her mind to practical use.

Although she knew a kiss was not required of her—being an unproductive use of one's time—she rose from her chair to buss her brother's cheek. Ravenwood had always been a very solemn, duty-oriented young man, but both his smiles and his presence had been far scarcer these past few months, ever since his childhood friends finally came home from war.

Some of them, that was. A black armband never failed to encircle Ravenwood's upper left arm. She fought the urge to hug him close. Were it not for having already inherited a dukedom, he would undoubtedly have followed his friends off to war.

Less certain was whether he would have made it home.

She walked to the fire to mask her shiver.

"Good morning, brother. To what do I owe the honor of this visit?" When he didn't join her before the fire, she turned to face him. "Is anything amiss?"

Ravenwood ran a hand through his wavy chestnut hair, upsetting the careful work of his valet.

Or not. Given the popularity of the "frightened owl" hairstyle today, Amelia couldn't fathom much effort being involved at all.

He glanced at the clock upon the mantel. "I hate to bother you with last minute changes—"

"Whatever the issue, have no fear. My plans are meticulous enough to withstand disruptions of any sort."

"Yes, well, even you could not have foreseen this disaster, and nothing will fix it. This afternoon's luncheon—"

Before he could complete this thought,

a knock sounded upon the parlor door.

With an apologetic smile, Amelia held up a brief finger to indicate the conversation would continue shortly. "One moment, I've been awaiting a messenger. Enter!"

One of the lead footmen slipped into the room, his face concerned. "I was unable to fetch Miss Azzara, my lady."

She raised a brow. "She was not at home?"

"Oh no, my lady. Were that the case, I would surely have awaited her return. I'm afraid Miss Azzara has contracted the mumps, and will not be able to perform today after all."

Ravenwood's mouth parted in surprise. "Miss Azzara of Drury Lane? You'd mentioned we would provide musical entertainment as part of today's luncheon, but I never dreamt you meant the second-most celebrated opera singer in all of London."

"A good thing, too, since it seems it shan't happen."

"Let this be a lesson, Amelia. No plan is too meticulous for unforeseen circumstances to derail."

She inclined her head to her brother and turned to address the footman. "Thank you. That will be all."

He bowed. But before he could quit the parlor, a second footman arrived. This one, in grand contrast, was all smiles.

"Package delivered, my lady. Butler put her in the rose parlor, with the pianoforte."

"Put...'her'?" Ravenwood echoed faintly.

"Miss Catalini," the footman explained. "She's to sing this afternoon. Her man is already practicing scales with her."

"Miss Angelica Catalini?" Ravenwood swung his head back toward Amelia. "The *first*-most celebrated opera singer in all of London?"

"We promised musical entertainment," she reminded him with a smile. She nodded to the footmen. "Thank you, gentlemen. You did well."

Ravenwood continued to stare at her. "You knew Miss Azzara would contract the mumps?"

"Of course not. As I have tried to impress upon you, a smart woman plans for every exigency."

He gestured at the footmen's retreating

backs. "And if both songstresses should have arrived?"

"Then they might have taken turns in sets, or performed a series of duets." She steepled her fingers. "Now it will simply be an exclusive."

Distant carriage wheels crunched upon the frozen gravel of the ducal drive.

Ravenwood turned to her in horror. "Early! I knew there was no time to change course, but cousin Blaylock can usually be counted upon to arrive a half hour late to any gathering. Under the circumstances, I would've supposed their pace to be even slower than usual, what with—"

"Don't make such a kick-up. 'Tis not our guests."

"But how can you—"

Two downstairs maids appeared at the still-open doorway, one with wringing hands and the other shooting her quick, bolstering looks.

"Peggy. Martha. Do come in."

Both maids rushed forward, nearly tripping over each other as they curtsied. The one with the ashen face spoke first.

"I know it's washing day, mum, and I'm

much needed here, but my niece is dreadful sick—"

"*Dreadful* sick," put in the second maid. "Hottest fever you ever did see, and her a moppet of not more than two years."

"It's not my day off until next week," the first maid continued, "but Peggy's is today, and she's offered to switch with me—"

"No problem at all, mum, not when I been there meself—got four cherubim of my own, y'know. All been sick at one time or another."

"If you'll say it's all right, that is." Martha wrung her hands. "She's just a baby, and as I can't afford a doctor—Not because of you, mum! Your wages are fairer than anyone! It's just that there's only my mama in the house, and we had to patch up a few holes for the winter—"

Ravenwood cut a wide-eyed glance at Amelia as if he'd never heard more convoluted storytelling in his life. And why would he? She imagined this was likely to be the first direct contact he'd had with the under-servants since...ever. The running of a household was a woman's job, and the running of this particular household had been her exclusive domain since their mother died, when Amelia was fourteen. If it had run like clockwork all this time, it was due to nothing less than her meticulous planning.

"Of course," she said to the maids. "Peggy, you may report to the laundry. Martha, a hack has just arrived for you and is waiting outside. In it, you will find a medical doctor, as well as a small parcel of children's books you might read to your invalid as she convalesces. Hurry now. Return only when the fever has broken, and not a moment sooner."

"Thank you! Thank you!" the maid gasped as she curtsied, then fairly flew down the hall.

Ravenwood gaped at Amelia. "You cannot expect me to believe that you summoned a hack, a surgeon, and a parcel of books on the off chance that someone's niece or nephew would take ill today."

"Don't be absurd. I had the news half an hour ago, and would've sent Martha on her way forthwith had she not been racing through the manor in search of someone to switch laundry days with her. Unless you object to the expense?"

That startled a laugh out of him. "Buy the girl a library of children's books if that's your wish. The only thing that surprises me is that those two maids were patently *un*surprised that you were not only aware of the problem, but had already put steps in place toward its solution."

"Why should they be surprised? As mistress of this household, it is my responsibility to keep it running smoothly. They expect nothing less and, frankly, I'm hurt that you would suppose otherwise."

"Hurt! You must know that I think you in possession of the finest mind in all of England. That doesn't mean I cannot marvel at it from time to time. Nor should you fly into a miff if one of these days, something does not go according to plan."

"Such as the reason you stalked in here in high dudgeon this morning?"

"I shall ignore the gibe about 'high dudgeon' and inform you of the problem at once, before another thirty servants march about like pawns upon your chessboard.

Cousin Blaylock had declined our invitation because his wife is increasing, but I've just got a note saying that they'll be arriving after all, and are only a posting-house away. They'll be here within the hour."

"That's hardly a catastrophe. He's the most kindhearted parson of my acquaintance, and his young wife is a dream."

"Did you not hear me say she's also increasing? Blaylock's note says she wishes to join us for luncheon, but her stomach cannot abide the sight or smell of fish. I'm guessing salmon is one of the very things the kitchens have spent the morning preparing."

"An exceedingly good guess." Salmon was her brother's favorite dish, and since he attended luncheons so infrequently, Amelia strove to always have it present when he did. "Just a moment, please."

Mrs. Brown, the housekeeper, hurried toward them from down the corridor. She dipped a curtsey when she reached the parlor. "You rang, my lady?"

Ravenwood narrowed his eyes at Amelia. "You rang? When did you ring? I've been standing right next to you!"

"She rang a quarter past, I'm afraid." The housekeeper's cheeks flushed. "There was a small to-do with Miss Catalini's tea, but it is all settled now."

"You did quite right by attending to our present guests first," Amelia thanked her warmly. "Now then. Please instruct the cook that we will substitute sirloin of beef instead of fish at luncheon today. The rest of the dishes will remain unchanged. I trust there will be no problem?"

"None at all, my lady. The beef is very nearly done already, and I must say it all smells delightful. Your guests will be quite pleased."

"Thank you, Mrs. Brown. That is all."

Ravenwood held up his hands. "When did you— How—?"

"The moment I read Aunt Blaylock's letter." Amelia gestured at the neatly stacked piles of correspondence atop the cherrywood table as she settled into her wingback chair. "Do have a seat."

He sank into the chair opposite as if he barely registered its presence. "Is there anything you don't know?"

Amelia laughed. "Reams of things. I

haven't the least idea how many attend Parliament, for example, or what the new issues will be for 1816. That is your domain. But I do consider it my responsibility to know everything there is to know about anything that could be considered *my* domain. I believe I am quite adept at the management of people and events."

His green eyes twinkled. "You've certainly managed me since the day I was born."

"I was but three years old when you were born," she protested. "I didn't start managing you for at least another year."

Before her brother could reply, the underbutler strode into the parlor with a tray bearing two biscuits and a single glass of port.

Ravenwood's shock gave way to humor. "You're drinking spirits now? I would too if I had to play puppet-master all day in this household. In fact, it's quite bad of you not to have at least ordered a matching glass for me. I do intend to steal one of those biscuits. Cinnamon raisin is my favorite."

The butler presented him with the tray. "For you, my lord."

Ravenwood cut his gaze to his sister. "You can't be serious."

She arched a brow. "As it happens, the staff is on standing order to bring this specific refreshment at once, should you enter the yellow parlor while I am managing my household duties."

The butler gave her a bow. "It would have been much sooner, my lady, had we not also been in the midst of seeing to Miss Catalini. I do beg your pardon."

"As do I. I love these biscuits." Ravenwood took an appreciative bite. "But why a glass of port?"

She widened her eyes. "So that you feel welcome in my little cave."

"That is to say, why so few biscuits and only one glass? Why not a dozen biscuits and the port decanter?"

She smiled wickedly. "So that you do not overstay your welcome."

He laughed and held up the glass in salute. "To the best sister a brother could have!"

She grinned back at him, thrumming with satisfaction.

Despite his levity, no one took duty

more seriously than the Duke of Ravenwood. He'd inherited the title whilst still at Eton and, like her, had spent the rest of his life devoted to exceeding expectations. In fact, the only duty she could think of that he hadn't thrown himself into wholeheartedly was his duty to beget an heir.

Her throat dried as her guilt came back. To beget an heir, he would first require a wife. And the most logical reason for her duty-oriented brother not to have acquired a bride was because he believed his first loyalty lay with his sister. Not just because she was (slightly) older and could have been married off years ago, but because her entire life consisted of running this household. If he were to marry, that job necessarily must go to his duchess—leaving Amelia in the cold.

Rubbish, of course, but just the sort of romantical reasoning her brother would come up with. There was only one way to disabuse him of such a loyal but wrongheaded notion. It was time to put off the inevitable. She loved sharing a home with her brother, but could not keep standing in the way of his future happiness.

She had to get a husband.

But where to begin? She stretched her slippered toes toward the fire as she considered the problem anew. Her thirtieth birthday was coming up fast—the day after Christmas! Good heavens. A young lady in her twenties sounded ever so much more marriageable than a spinster in her thirties. Nothing for it. She'd simply have to bring a suitor up to scratch before Boxing Day.

She reached for a large leather volume that always rested within easy reach of her correspondence: *Debrett's Peerage*. The perfect resource for thinning the chaff. A fortnight should be plenty of time to make a selection.

Her brother glanced up from his second and final biscuit. "What are you reading?"

"Catalog."

As expected, his attention immediately returned to savoring the last biscuit. If that was the pinnacle of happiness in the man's life, then by God, was he in want of wife! She would turn her mind to him next, but not until she was no longer his perceived responsibility.

She opened the *Peerage* to the first page.

The book did not include likenesses of the peers of the realm, but physical beauty was not something that interested her. Nor was the state of a man's coffers. She would bring her husband a sizable dowry, made all the more impressive due to her having removed it from the five percents at a young age, choosing her own stocks for the principal and investing the interest elsewhere. The already grand sum had tripled over the past decade alone.

It was time to find someone to spend it on. She flipped through the pages. Earls, marquesses, dukes...What was her pleasure?

She had, of course, studied the matter thoroughly. A title was important insofar as planning for the futures of any offspring. Young people who were called Lady This and Lord That quite simply had more advantages than those who were not. Which meant barons and viscounts need not apply.

Nor would it do to be *bored*. While the gold in her husband's pockets was immaterial, a large household was paramount. While her spouse was off doing lordly things, she would pit her wits toward restructuring their household as efficiently as possible. Once it fairly ran itself, she would set about providing heirs, who would doubtlessly offer a lifetime's worth of situations to be managed. Just think of all the strange new problems she'd be likely to face! Absolutely brilliant.

"That's not a catalog." Her brother set aside his empty glass and plate to peer across the maplewood table. "Why the devil are you reading *Debrett's Peerage*?"

"It most certainly is a catalog, and the most expedient one at my disposal. I've decided to take a husband. His name must be within these pages."

"You can't husband-hunt in a book!"

"Perhaps you cannot. I intend to make a sensible match. How do you feel about the Duke of Lambley? Relations of his are diplomats somewhere in China. I can't think of anything more practical than a marital alliance with ties to the Silk Road."

"Lambley?" Ravenwood exploded. "I forbid you from even considering an unrepentant rake such as—What am I saying? Do not suck me into your stratagems, Machiavelli. I will not be involved."

"Machiavelli was a narrow-minded egoist, and I'll thank you not to compare us a second time. I should be shocked to discover 'self-centered' among the words that best describe me."

"Don't fly into one of your starts, I was just quizzing you. If you were at all self-centered, it wouldn't have taken you thirty years to come up with the idea of getting married."

"Twenty-nine, puppy!"

"Nonetheless, while I recognize that I cannot fathom by what means you realize your various plans, I cannot think that one's life love is to be found within the pages of a book."

She snorted. "*You* might be susceptible to poetry and long walks in the garden. Falling in love is for people who don't know how to plan. But if you insist I apply my efforts toward men I already know, I shall choose from among your friends. The Earl of Carlisle might do. I hear his estate is an absolute nightmare."

"You stay away from the dukes of war!" he thundered. "I would not have any one of them toss their handkerchief at my sister."

Dukes of war, indeed. Trust Ravenwood to coin such a flowery phrase—and use it so disparagingly. "I thought they were your closest friends?"

His eyes shuttered. "They were."

"Ease your mind. I'm not a debutante whose head is turned by a pretty face and smart regimentals. I'm looking for someone less...elemental." She held up the *Peerage*. "I obviously won't know which of these fine gentlemen is to be my future husband for at least another week, but you cannot deny it is an excellent resource for trimming the names down to a manageable list."

"And *then* what? Gad about knocking on doors?"

"Of course not! First impressions are key. Which means an elaborate gown, an intricate hairstyle, and dim ballroom lighting."

Ravenwood leaned back in his chair. "Are you saying you'll contrive to get all these paragons of eligible bachelorhood under one roof?"

"That unparalleled efficiency has already been done for me. In twelve days, everyone in this book will be at the Sheffields' seventy-fifth annual Christmas Eve ball." She set down the *Peerage* in order to flip through the tallest stack of correspondence. She frowned when she could not easily find what she sought. "The invitation must be in here somewhere...Viscount Sheffield always sends them out by the first of December, and today is the twelfth."

"Well, you're half right. Today is the twelfth. But there's not going to be a seventy-fifth annual Christmas Eve ball this year."

"What do you mean, 'this year'? This is the only year he can have a seventy-fifth annual ball. Next year would be the seventy-sixth, which won't count a button if he skips years willy-nilly in-between."

Ravenwood shook his head. "Not willy-nilly. Canceling wasn't his choice."

"Oh, stuff. He's only the viscount, and the sole master of his affairs. Does the holiday conflict with his pleasuring this year? I've heard he's quite a rattle for hunting parties or Gentleman Jackson's. Don't tell me he'd rather spend the evening at some gaming hell than continue tradition."

"I can't rightly say where he'd rather be, but the man loves parties. A stroke of lightning took the matter right out of his hands. You can claim his family's holiday party as a London institution all you wish, but the orchestra stage is nothing more than ashes and the whole of the interior stinks of smoke."

"When did this occur?" she demanded. "I didn't hear a word."

"A fortnight ago. He kept it out of the papers. Between the weather and the holidays, renovation won't be completed until spring."

She sniffed. "I'm sure *I* could have had it ready by Christmas, had I been consulted when the incident first occurred."

Her brother laughed. "You mean if you had any say whatsoever in Viscount Sheffield's business? In any case, it's too late now. You said it yourself—even *you* couldn't restore the venue in time for Christmas."

She arched a brow. "Who said the soirée

needs to take place in the same old ballroom? All we need is a new venue."

"*We?*" Ravenwood reared back, horrified.

"Not you, dear brother. Viscount Sheffield and I."

"Does the poor flat even know who you are?" Ravenwood burst out.

Her smile turned calculating. "He's about to."

"It's impossible!" Her brother gestured wildly. "It's not just a question of venue. It's finding a great number of staff to work the holiday, an exorbitant amount of food, an army of chefs to prepare it, an orchestra for dancing, any number of other entertainments, all at the last minute, then sending out handwritten invitations to everyone in that cursed book of yours informing them of the new details and praying they haven't made alternate plans..." He shook his head. "I'm sorry, Amelia. It would take more than a miracle. There's only twelve days left."

She pushed to her feet. "Then there's no time to lose."

CHAPTER 2

Benedict St. John, Viscount Sheffield, had a complicated relationship with his pocket watch.

He wasn't married to it, of course. Besides being a silly notion, he still held the same view on marriage as he had for the past five-and-thirty years: Not yet. He simply had no *time* for a wife.

No, the problem—or the joy, depending on one's vantage point—of his relationship with his pocket watch was that eight o'clock occurred twice a day. Benedict cleaved to that magic number, for it demarcated two very different aspects of his life.

From eight in the morning to eight in the evening, he was focused, take-no-prisoners Lord Sheffield, with nary a second's thought spared on women or horseflesh or merrymaking. At precisely eight in the evening, however, the sands shifted.

Woe betide the fool who brought business matters to Benedict's ears during the precious hours when he distanced himself from the relentless weight of his duties as lord! For as assiduously as he focused his entire being on taxes and tenants and politics and land during his working hours, he threw himself just as wholly and as recklessly into mind-numbing entertainments during his evening hours.

It was the only way he *could* be breakfasted and at his desk by eight of the clock every single morning. He just had to throw every fiber of his being into his affairs until the clock tolled eight, whereupon he could finally throw every fiber of his being into his...well, also his affairs. The more pleasurable kind. Which he oughtn't be thinking about at the moment, because there was almost half an hour of office time left. If he kept his mind sharp, he could balance one more table of accounts before heading to the theater, where he intended to select a new mistress for a private season of off-stage performances.

Accounts. Right. Focusing, he dipped his pen into the standish and began totaling the first row of sums. He made it through the first few pages before his butler appeared in the doorway.

Benedict frowned. *No one* called upon him during working hours without prior arrangement. "Yes, Coombs?"

"I'm afraid there's a Lady Amelia Pembroke here to see you, my lord. She was most insistent."

"I trust you informed her that I was not receiving, and refused to let her in?"

"Of course." Coombs hesitated before continuing, "She said she would simply wait until you are receiving."

Benedict put down his pen. "Wait where, pray?"

"Upon the front step, my lord. I'm afraid the lady brought...the lady brought...a *book*. She cannot be budged."

Benedict tilted his head, impressed. Rather than attempt to barge her way in, she'd come prepared to wait him out—on the front stair, where every eye in every townhouse in the whole crescent was likely watching her. Intrigued despite himself, he tugged at his fob and checked the time on his watch.

A quarter 'til eight. Damn.

"Did the lady mention whether she was calling for business or for pleasure?"

"Both, my lord."

He coughed. "Both?"

"She would not elaborate. She said...she said explaining the intricacies of her design to a butler would be a waste of both our valuable time, and that each of us would operate far more efficiently minding the tasks in which we're experienced. Then she pulled out a book and a pair of spectacles and sat down on the front step to read."

Benedict mentally canceled his plans for the theater. He loved actresses, found them endlessly diverting in fact, but was forced to admit he'd never once been *intrigued* by one. They were beautiful, simple creatures, which was precisely what he liked about them. After a long day of arguing in the House of Lords or negotiating business contracts or managing tenant properties, he liked to disconnect his brain and let the rest of his body reign for a few hours.

At least, he'd always thought he liked that. He was beginning to suspect he liked being intrigued even more. He consulted the hour again.

Still a quarter to eight.

A sudden thought occurred to him. "Do you mean to say we've got a *lady* with her derrière freezing to ice atop our slush-covered concrete?"

Coombs shook his head. "Not at all, my lord. She brought several rugs and a warming brick, and had her coachman clear off the steps before she settled in. He's got eyes on her, even if he can't talk her back into the carriage."

Benedict drummed his fingers atop his leg. She hadn't just been prepared in case she had to wait—she'd known it would happen! She'd planned for the lost time, for the denied entry, for the slush upon the stoop, for the inclement weather...

He shoved his watch back into his pocket.

Business *and* pleasure, the chit had said.

He certainly hoped so. “By all means, Coombs. Show the intrepid lady in.”

He returned to his sums until footsteps sounded out in the corridor. Eight o’clock. Perfect timing. He sheathed his pen.

Let the games begin.

He pushed to his feet the moment the lady appeared in his doorway.

Her hair was a rich brown and her eyes a clear green, but despite the fine cut of her gown or the becoming flush upon her cheekbones, those were not the aspects of her appearance he found the most incredible.

She was *dry*.

There wasn’t a spot of snow on her pristine slippers. No hint of dampness to her velvet-and-ermine pelisse. No sign of the book or the warming brick or the infamous rugs. She had not only planned to be kept out, she had also planned to be let in!

“Who *are* you?” he found himself asking, his tone at complete odds with his usual charm and decorum.

She dipped a pretty curtsey. “Oh dear, I have you at sixes and sevens. I am Lady Amelia Pembroke, sister of Lawrence Pembroke, whom you perhaps better known as the Duke of Ravenwood."

He peered behind her. "Where is your chaperone?"

"*Elder* sister," she enunciated crisply. "At nine-and-twenty, I find myself *being* a chaperone rather than requiring one. If you suspect I have come to trap you to the altar, have no fear. Once our brief partnership has concluded, you will have no need to lay eyes on me anew. In fact, interacting in person need not happen beyond just this once. It would be far more efficient for us both if I were allowed to handle our business from here on out."

He leaned back. "What, may I ask, is the nature of our business?"

She inclined her head. "Just so. It came to my attention earlier today that you had canceled the seventy-fifth annual Christmas Eve ball. I would have called upon you immediately, but I'm afraid a prior engagement tied my hands until this very moment."

He tried to make sense of her words. She was apologizing for not descending upon him more promptly for a meeting he'd never in his wildest dreams anticipated?

"I didn't cancel it," he found himself protesting. "The ballroom burned down. There's nowhere to *have* a party."

She beamed at him. "So you agree!"

He blinked. "I agree with what?"

"That the problem is the venue, not the soirée. It's settled, then. You may return to your business. I shall handle all the arrangements. We'll be ready to announce the new location by the end of the week."

"We...What new location?"

"I haven't decided yet, of course. I didn't wish to undertake any investigations until having spoken with you. Not only would that have been presumptuous, it would have been a shocking waste of time if you and I weren't in agreement that the party must not be canceled."

He shook his head. "We're in agreement?"

"Wonderful." She clasped her hands together. "Now, lest you think I am in any way out to swindle you, let's have done with the subject of money once and for all. Neither of us hurt for coin, so in the interest of expediency, I am prepared to finance this year's soirée from my own pocket. You're a very busy man, and I am certain you wouldn't wish me to hound your doorstep at all hours of the day, begging for pin money for this florist or that sous chef."

"No, of course I...*Stop.*" He held a finger close to her lips. "No—don't open your pretty mouth until I've had a moment to think."

She returned his gaze with the most placid of expressions. He wasn't quizzed for a moment.

As he considered his extraordinary guest, it belatedly occurred to him that he'd forgotten to bow. Well, it was too late for that. The introductions, such as they were, had done. But it wasn't too late to take hold of this quickly deteriorating situation before it spiraled completely out of hand.

He hoped.

Lady Amelia was apparently so determined that his family party take place, she was willing to organize it herself and finance the entire endeavor. Unfortunately for her, those were the two arguments least likely to sway his mind. Unlike most peers, Benedict had inherited his title not from his father, but from a distant uncle. He had not been raised with the expectation of inheriting so much as a shilling, much less groomed for the role of viscount. He hadn't even been next in line. One day he'd been a happy-go-lucky poor relation, and the next he was attending a mass funeral after a devastating outbreak of scarlet fever.

Everything he knew about the viscountcy, he'd had to teach himself. Everything he now owned, every penny the estate was now worth, came from ten years of hard work. If there was one thing he was constitutionally unable to do, it was relinquish any control of his hard won self-sufficiency. And there was perhaps nothing more closely entrenched in the viscountcy itself as the annual Christmas Eve ball.

If there was a second thing he was constitutionally unable to do, it was allow some other *parti* to finance any aspect of his personal or business affairs. To allow outside help might suggest Benedict unable to perform his duties, but to incur a debt of any kind would *prove* it.

Plainly speaking, there was no chance in hell Lady Amelia would get her way.

On the other hand, it was after eight o'clock at night and Benedict saw no point in longwinded explanations or upsetting the lady. The best course of action was to act receptive until after she quit his townhouse, and then send an elegant note of apology on the morrow, indicating (in writing!) that after thinking it over, he had no wish to pursue the holiday party, nor was there any need for her further involvement. There. It was settled. He had only to humor her until then.

"That is a very interesting proposal," he said aloud, careful to keep his smile engaging but his tone noncommittal. "If we were to pursue such a route, where would you relocate the festivities?"

Her response was brisk. "The most obvious choice is Ravenwood House, my brother's Hyde Park estate. While most aristocratic families winter in townhouses just like this one, I don't believe I'm exaggerating if I say that the ducal grounds boast the same square footage as this entire crescent. While nothing can replace what you've lost, the Ravenwood ballroom can certainly accommodate the correct number of guests in a comparable level of luxury and style."

He was no longer surprised to hear she had a ready, well-reasoned answer. If anything, he was pleasantly surprised to find himself capable of scotching it.

"As generous as your offer is, I cannot accept it. I'm certain it is the sin of pride at play, but I could not in good conscience allow a Sheffield ball to take place under the Ravenwood roof. The guests would quite properly consider it the first annual Ravenwood ball, which, as it happens, is not a poor idea. Why don't you pursue that instead?"

"Because it is at odds with my goals. I have put together many successful events over the years, but frankly, no invitation carries the prestige and sense of tradition like one with 'Seventy-fifth Annual' embossed across the top. My soirées are well-attended. But yours? No one wishes to miss a fête their family has attended for three generations."

He tried to look sympathetic. "In that

case, I am very sorry that it didn't work out."

She frowned. "Of course it will work out. All we've done is agree that it cannot be at your estate, and it cannot be at mine."

"You *agree* that it cannot be at Ravenwood House?"

"'Tis not my party. The location deserved to be mentioned, however, since it *is* the most convenient. Which brings us to independent venues. The expense of finding and staffing such a location is much greater at this late date, but the advantages are threefold. First, it is a neutral location, untainted by any other family's title. Second, the very fact of not being a traditional ballroom increases the possibilities for alternate forms of entertainment, which will be an even bigger draw to your guests. Third, choosing a fashionable location will ensure the attendance of those who wish to see and be seen. The more attractive the entertainment and the easier it is to attend, the greater the chance of realizing the entire guest list."

Another rational, well-thought-out answer. He crossed his arms. "Why are you doing this?"

She smiled benignly. "I manage things. You have a project that needs managing."

His spine snapped up straight. "I'm quite capable of managing my own affairs. I've done so for the ten years I've been viscount—"

"Yes, yes, and you've done a marvelous job." She patted his arm. "No one is doubting your ability to improve upon tradition and somehow make every year's Christmas Eve ball even better than the last. What I do doubt is that you have the next fortnight free to do nothing more than apply yourself to relocating this year's soirée without sacrificing any of the cachet."

"Exactly! I love Christmas and deplore the idea of breaking tradition, but I already devote twelve hours a day to far more pressing matters, and cannot possibly drive myself mad undertaking something so easily skipped." He crossed his arms. "The ball may be a highlight of the season, but it's necessarily a low priority. It's as simple as that."

She tapped a finger to her cheek. "Are you...laboring under the misapprehension that you are debating me? To my ears, it sounds very much like we are arguing the same side. You want the holiday party. I want the holiday party. You don't have time to devote to it. I have all the time in the world. What am I missing?"

"That I don't want *you* to do it," he blurted out. "I don't need your money, nor do I wish my family tradition to be altered by someone who is not family."

"Ah. Why didn't you say so at once? That's the easiest of all things to resolve."

He blinked. "How?"

"You'll pay for every penny of it, of course. You'll have full approval of the venue. And I'll submit a change request log to you every morning in writing, to which you can respond by dashing quick checks or Xs next to each line."

A rushing sound filled his ears. "Change...request...log?"

"I have attended every one of your Christmas Eve balls since my come-out twelve years ago." She held up a hand. "No —don't apologize for not recognizing me.

It is the one time a year we are under the same roof, and they are infamously glorious crushes. You'll be pleased to know that I took extensive notes every single year, and am reasonably confident that if your venue had not burned down, I could have recreated the exact experience to a button."

He stared at her. "You took extensive notes? On my holiday parties?"

"I would've been foolish not to. I was mistress of my brother's ducal estate by then, and what better example to copy than the most celebrated fête of the year?" She waved a hand in the air. "My point is that I, of all people, am uniquely qualified to not only follow your family traditions as closely as possible without draining your time with direct supervision, but I can also recognize when elements must be unavoidably altered, and provide you with a detailed list in plenty of time for final decision-making."

He couldn't believe his ears. "Christmas Eve is two weeks away! How is that plenty of time?"

"Twelve days, to be precise. I doubt I

will require half of that if money is no object, and you respond to my daily missives within...three hours. Does that sound like an efficient plan?"

He narrowed his eyes at the casually dropped *three hours*. He'd bet his left arm that, if asked, she could recite compelling reasons why three—not two and not four—hours was ideal turnabout. He was equally certain that she'd purposefully framed her final yes-or-no question as asking whether he believed the concept to be efficient, instead of whether he wished to go forward with it.

Clever, clever girl.

"How about I let you know what I think after I've had a chance to consider these independent venues, as you put it. I suppose you have that chosen as well?"

"Not at all. I have narrowed it down to three. I won't be able to provide you with a recommendation until I have visited them all, with an eye specifically turned to replicating your family tradition as faithfully as possible whilst taking advantage of the new location's unique assets."

"I see. And I suppose you intend to start on this first thing in the morning?"

"I intend to make significant progress in the next few minutes. My coachman is awaiting me outside because my next engagement begins promptly at nine. You can expect my report on the Theatre Royal to arrive sometime before dawn."

The theatre. His lips quirked. How ironic. "And if I wished to be present on this investigative expedition?"

She arched a brow. "Do you?"

He was startled to find that he did. "I do."

"Then grab your coat. They're expecting us backstage within the hour."

CHAPTER 3

Benedict eased down from his carriage onto the slick winter street and strode just in front to the Ravenwood coach, where its tiger was opening the door for the intriguing lady inside. Benedict stepped between the groom and the open door, and offered his own arm to help Lady Amelia out of the coach. The fact that she likely didn't need his or anyone's assistance only made him less willing to let go. Her potent mix of brains and beauty was difficult to resist. He half-marveled that she had not had the foresight to contract all the street sweeps of London to clear the ice from the curb leading to the theatre door.

Then again, given her polite but firm

set-down to his butler, the lady was likely to view such an extravagance as an inefficient use of the street sweepers' time.

Lady Amelia rested one gloved hand in the crook of Benedict's arm and used the other to raise her skirts a safe distance from the inch of slush coating the muddy streets. He was treated to a brief flash of shapely ankles and leather half-boots—the same ones she'd undoubtedly worn whilst reading her novel on his front stoop. On the other hand, was this woman truly the sort to "waste" time on a novel?

He tucked her closer to his side as they hurried toward the theatre entrance. He hunched against the icy breeze out of habit. He'd ceased feeling cold the second Lady Amelia's fingers curved about his arm. "My butler informs me you had a book on your person when you came to call."

She did not look up. "His vision is excellent, my lord."

"Was it your journal?" he pressed. He wondered if she kept a diary as well...and what she might write about him. He hoped something scandalous. He'd love to make it come true. "With your notes on my holiday parties?"

"Journals, plural." Her clear green eyes met his. "And, no, it was not."

"Journals, *plural*?" This new intelligence was so startling that he completely abandoned all interest in whatever tome she'd brought earlier. "How many can you possibly have?"

"Five, plus a slimmer volume for indexing each cross-reference. All six are in the carriage, should you wish to verify their comprehensiveness for yourself."

"There is no need." He did not doubt their presence. What he could not comprehend was what the devil she'd managed to say about his parties for five indexed journals. "Did you carry parchment and ink with you about the ballroom?"

The corners of her plump rosy lips quirked. "That would be highly impractical."

"To be sure! Then how did you remember whatever on earth it is that you have annotated in five journals?"

Her eyes widened. "I stored the details

in my memory pantry. As I fully intend to do tonight."

An usher swung open the doors to the theatre and bustled them out of the cold and into the gilded reception hall.

Benedict scarcely noted the sudden warmth, so intent was he on the tranquil woman at his side. "In your *what*?"

"My memory pantry." She eased into one of the plush lobby chairs to accept a fresh change of shoes from her groom.

Benedict tried not to be distracted by the much longer glimpses of her silk-stockinged ankles.

She handed her sodden half-boots to her groom then turned her piercing gaze back to Benedict. "There are twenty-six fruits, for example. A is for Apple, B is for Blackberry, and so on. I memorize facts by picturing each new detail with a pantry item. The sillier the juxtaposition, the better. It's no challenge at all to recall vivid imagery later."

"No challenge at—Yes. Thank you." He relinquished his greatcoat to the usher and accepted his own change of footwear from his tiger. The lady was ingenious! "That is quite a trick. Even so, I cannot credit that five journals can spawn from twenty-six images, no matter how vivid."

"Memory *pantry,* my lord. Not memory *shelf.*" She brushed out her skirts. "Those were the fruits. My pantry also contains vegetables, meats, drinks, pies... More than enough to fill a simple journal. I daresay I'll run out of facts to record before I run out of ingredients to assign them to."

Incredible. He offered her his arm. He would not be letting her go any time soon. "But—"

Before he could complete his question, the theatre manager himself appeared in the lobby and lowered himself in a deep bow. "Lady Amelia! Lord Sheffield! I am honored to provide a small tour of the theatre. I would love to show you about for as long as you wish, but the next show begins in an hour, and I cannot postpone the performance. Patrons have already begun to arrive."

Amelia nodded thoughtfully. "How much money would it take for you to agree to do so?"

"Cancel the show?" the manager gasped.

"Now? Tonight? But it is Grimaldi himself, in *Robinson Crusoe*!"

"Not tonight," she said soothingly. "Christmas Eve. Could you reschedule that to another time?"

"Could I reschedule—*Christmas Eve*—" the manager choked, his face purpling.

She spoke more slowly. "Is there a performance scheduled for that evening?"

"Yes, of course! Since the theatre is closed on Christmas, Grimaldi's last performance as Friday is to be that evening, and Miss O'Neill will be reprising her role as Juliet earlier that afternoon. I couldn't possibly—"

"Splendid. By simply moving Mr. Grimaldi's performance one day forward, we have solved all logistics without any hassle. Mind you, we still haven't decided if we will select this establishment. We're simply ensuring there are no impediments."

"But Lady Amelia, *Grimaldi!* The gentry can have no argument with postponing at your ladyship's convenience, but—the dukes! The earls! 'Tis impossible, my lady."

"They won't have to alter their plans one whit," she replied calmly. "'Twould be a different event, but held at the same time and place. I can't think of anything more convenient to our needs."

The manager sent an imploring look in Benedict's direction.

Benedict could do little more than lift a shoulder in empathy. It was plainly apparent that if Lady Amelia set her mind to bringing about a given circumstance, no force on earth could slow her down.

"Come now," she said briskly. "The next performance begins in less than an hour. I believe you wished to give us a brief tour of the less public areas?"

"Yes, I...Of course, of course." He bowed. "My lady had enquired about evacuation routes in the event of a fire, and what steps must be taken to ensure hot foods are served hot, and cold dishes cold."

Benedict stared at her. "Are you this exacting every time you go to the theatre?"

"Don't be absurd. I *am* fastidious when the responsibility for my guests' safety and enjoyment falls upon my shoulders. Your shoulders, that is." She fixed him with wide green eyes and a slow blink of thick chestnut lashes. "We can skip safety and enjoyment if you like?"

He tucked her hand closer to his side. "By all means, madam. Let's have our inspection."

In short order, he found himself intimately acquainted with the proscenium arch (opulent), the stage floor (enormous), the dining possibilities (atrocious), the actresses (lovely), and the famous harlequin Joseph Grimaldi himself (an unparalleled genius).

"Do say we're staying for his performance," he murmured into Lady Amelia's ear. Her skin smelled of rosewater. He leaned closer, then jolted upright when he realized he'd all but asked for permission, as if he were leg-shackled to the chit instead of gammoning her until he could cancel upon the morrow.

To her credit, Lady Amelia raised no brow over the gaffe, and responded with an indifference that rankled worse than toadeating. "You may do as you wish, of course. Since I've only previously viewed the stage from the private Ravenwood box, I haven't the least notion of the sightline or acoustics from the side balconies, front galleries, parterre, or lower stalls. I shall stay just long enough to note the differences in sight, sound, and general comfort from each strategic location."

"Just long enough to—" He didn't bother to hide his amusement. "In other words, you don't intend to relax and enjoy the performance?"

She stared at him as if she'd never heard the terms *relax* and *enjoy* before in her life. It was more than a little concerning.

"Of course not." She turned toward the stairs leading to the highest boxes. "Once the performance begins, it should only require a few moments in each locality to ascertain its suitableness as a vantage point. I should be home in bed with my report already dashed off to you in a matter of hours."

"Your report to *me*?" he repeated, trying not to picture her reclining in a bed. "Aren't I standing right here with you?"

Her brow knitted. "Clearly. But my notes will be an invaluable resource once we've multiple venues to compare."

He shook his head in disbelief. "No."

She bristled. "Of course they—"

"Obviously your report will be the finest and most comprehensive treatise ever written about the Theatre Royal on the subject of ballroom appropriateness and guest safety. But as the manager said—it's Grimaldi! He makes an astonishing Friday." Benedict laid his hands upon her arms in sudden realization. "Have you never attended *Robinson Crusoe* for fun?"

"Fun?" she repeated blankly. She tilted a baffled gaze up at him. "Why would I do that?"

Why, indeed. He stared at her with something akin to horror. Had he been feeling sorry for himself for ten long years of twelve-hour workdays? He far preferred his stolen hours of mindless entertainments to the idea of never being entertained at all. It was pitiable, really, that a woman this clever should not know what it was to disconnect her wits for a moment to simply enjoy the world about her. Something ought to be done! And he was just the man to do it.

Deuce take it, the fetching Lady Amelia

needed him even more desperately than the Christmas ball needed her.

Which, he recognized wryly, meant he was going through with her party scheme. He smiled. It also meant he had twelve nights to teach Lady Amelia to enjoy life.

"How can you say with certainty whether any activity delivers the proper level of guest delight, if you do not allow yourself to experience pleasure for pleasure's sake?"

She blinked.

He grinned, inordinately pleased with himself for having phrased *come enjoy this evening with me* in such a way that she could not possibly refuse. "I shall permit you to drag me all over Town in search of the perfect venue if you allow me the pleasure of escorting you about said venue, with a goal no more profound than to enjoy whatever pleasures the location has to offer."

She pursed her rosy lips. "These are the terms of your acceptance?"

"Indeed."

"Very well." She sighed. "Shocking waste of time, but at least there are only two more left to visit."

He smiled at the challenge in her eyes. Silly chit. He'd already won.

He could not attend to her during the days, of course—rules were rules, and his daytime hours were already spoken for. His evenings, however...The lady didn't know it yet, but for the next fortnight, his evenings belonged to her. They would both part ways richer for the experience. He would enjoy an unbroken streak of Christmastide soirées, and she...

She would be introduced to pleasure.

CHAPTER 4

Amelia glanced at the clock on her mantel and frowned. Half past eight. She would have to leave in the next few moments if she were to make tonight's meeting at the appointed hour. But Lord Sheffield had yet to arrive, and it was imperative that he accompany her. She'd been looking forward to another battle of wits.

Her mouth tightened. When he hadn't responded to her detailed treatise on the Theatre Royal, she had been heartened, not dismayed. He was a man of action. If he meant to scotch her scheme, he would have done. Therefore, he meant to join her. Her missive had clearly stated her intent to set off for the next venue no later than—

"My lady?"

The butler! Her shoulders relaxed. "Yes?"

"Lord Sheffield has come to call. I've put him in the blue sitting room."

"Splendid." She pushed away her pen and standish. Tomorrow would be soon enough for addressing invitations. She scooped up her pelisse and swept downstairs to greet the viscount.

He started to see her dressed for the winter. "I thought you were not going!"

"However did you take such a notion? The missive I sent at breakfast indicated my departure for the next tour would be promptly at half eight. I should hope I haven't done anything in our short acquaintance to give you any cause to doubt my word."

"But I didn't respond to your missive! The snow made traffic plod, and when I did not see your carriage out front awaiting your departure, I thought I had missed you altogether and wasted the trip. But when your butler said no, his lady was upstairs working, I could only assume—"

"Then you make quite ridiculous assumptions, indeed."

"As do you, my lady. The Theatre Royal, while boasting all the fine qualities listed in your six-page document, is not an option. I am not so full of my own self-importance that I would callously cancel hundreds of families' Christmastide plans, just for me to throw a party."

"Then you will adore tonight's venue. I chose it just for that reason." She tilted her head toward the door. "Are we ready?"

He stared at her, incredulous. "Ready? I haven't a clue where we're going!"

"Haven't you?" she teased. "But it's Wednesday!"

"*Almack's*?" His mouth opened and shut without making a sound. "But its rooms are only open during the Season, which hasn't even begun yet—"

"—making it quite suitable for our ends. All we have to do is bend the patronesses to our point of view. Lady Jersey has agreed to hear our request."

"Bend—*Queen Sarah*—" He burst into laughter and offered her his arm. "Come, my lady. I shall permit you to do all the talking."

She slipped her gloved fingers into the

crook of his elbow and allowed him to escort her to his waiting carriage. Despite the many times her societal roles had caused her to be on the arm of this duke or that earl, she had never before been struck by the sudden, foolish wish that her fingers were not so properly gloved, and his arm not so encased in winter layers, so that she might feel the warmth and strength of the muscle beneath.

Heat pricked the back of her neck. *Her*, blush? It simply would not do.

Oh, certainly, Lord Sheffield was a Tulip of Fashion and a delight for the eyes. Even were he to suddenly attire himself in waistcoats of tangerine and puce, his golden curls and sparkling hazel eyes would flutter the heart of any maiden—and did. Amelia was not so green as to be unaware of his rakish reputation. Being alone with him in a carriage might be considered fast, even if one was a spinster in her dotage.

And yet...His behavior toward her had spoken very well of him from the very first. When he had enquired about her chaperonage, *she* had been the one to point out her age obviated the necessity. He had not only been perfectly willing to drive separately to their various assignations, he had accepted the assumption without question. It was *she* who had foregone her carriage in favor of accompanying the viscount.

Just what were her intentions toward the man? She bit her lip and forced herself to turn from his handsome mien and focus instead on the view out the carriage window.

His profile reflected back at her.

She closed her eyes. It wouldn't do, she reminded herself. Besides the frivolous reasons that they could not suit—his estate being perfectly run, future children failing to be lords and ladies—his nightly carousing was legendary, and unlikely to alter for someone as negligible as a wife.

Unless the rumors were greatly exaggerated? She indulged herself in another long look at the golden-haired Corinthian seated across from her. He didn't *seem* blue-deviled and bleary-eyed. But if that was because he'd spent the entirety of his daylight hours sleeping off a night of unrepentant bacchanalia, then she couldn't even fathom a friendship forming between them.

No. She'd had it from no less than three sources: after she'd gone home from the theatre at two in the morning, he'd traipsed directly to the Daffy Club, where he'd caroused until dawn.

His eyes met hers and his brows lifted in question.

She gazed back blandly, thankful the shadowed interior would mask any flush to her cheeks.

"Guinea for your thoughts," he said in his low, smooth voice.

"Prinny has caused that much inflation?"

The corners of his mouth quirked. "Most people's ruminations aren't worth a ha' penny. Yours, I am persuaded, are worth considerably more."

"You shan't think so once I've made them known." She flattened her lips into a straight line. "I was thinking about those who behave impractically. All of today's scandal sheets were full of a certain Viscount S—'s adventures with Blue Ruin."

She arched a brow pointedly. "Late night, was it?"

"Mmm. And an early morning." He stretched his long legs out before him. "As a lady of clocklike precision yourself, you may appreciate my schedule. I have kept strictly to it every day for the past decade. From eight in the morning to eight in the evening, I devote myself to my duties. Then from eight in the evening to eight in the morning, *I...do...not.*" He smiled, as if in remembrance of some unspeakable exploit.

Amelia was horrified. His devil-may-care response had been crafted in just such a way to provoke her displeasure, and so it had. But not, perchance, for the reasons he might expect.

As much as she tired of the house parties and winter retreats she was obliged to attend, or the two weeks in Bath every year with her cousins the Kingsleys, she could not deny the rejuvenating effect of several days in a row without a single responsibility or effort on her part. While she'd been picnicking at follies or riding in the parks, he hadn't enjoyed a single ray of sunshine at all.

She bit her lip. His estate might run smoothly, but it was in shocking want of efficiency. What had he said about the Christmastide party? He hadn't wanted *her* to do it?

"Requiring help does not indicate one is incapable of performing a task," she said softly. "It simply means it is more expedient not to do so."

The darkling look he glowered upon her could have melted iron.

They were both saved from what was likely to be a lively row by arriving on King Street. Lord Sheffield sprang from the carriage before the great wheels had completely settled, but reached up at once to hand her down.

She was appalled to shiver not at the blustery chill but at the breadth of his shoulders and the strength of his arms. Many a sillier maiden had tumbled down just this path. She was made of sterner stuff. Much more *sensible* stuff. She and the viscount were involuntary coconspirators until the conclusion of his party, and not a whisper more.

Dipping their heads against the wind,

they hurried to the entrance. Despite Almack's having been closed for months, a footman stood at the ready to push open the door and collect their coats. There was no way to know whether he worked here year-round, or had been summoned specifically for their meeting. Perhaps he was one of Lady Jersey's grooms. Amelia had recognized the crest upon the carriage in front of theirs.

Just as Amelia was shaking out her skirts, Lady Jersey strode up to greet them, flanked by a passel of maids and footmen.

After paying their respects, the countess turned her sharp brown eyes to Lord Sheffield. "I'm given to understand the Christmas Eve ball has not been canceled after all?"

He lifted a hand in Amelia's direction. "It seems everything Lady Amelia sets her mind to, happens."

The countess gave Amelia a nod of approval. "Ladies do know best about such things. I would not offer the services of Almack's to just anyone—and I've yet to mention the scheme to my fellow patronesses whose unreserved approval is, of course, necessary—but as we are not yet in Season, and the annual Sheffield ball is the largest and most prestigious of all the winter galas, you may be assured it is no surprise whatever that after lightning destroyed your ballroom, the first and only alternate location that sprang to mind was Almack's."

Lord Sheffield slanted Amelia a wry look. She blinked back at him innocently.

"You both have held vouchers for your entire adult lives, so I need not point out the splendor of the ballroom or the convenience of our supper rooms. You are well acquainted with what makes Almack's the best and most exclusive venue in the city. Follow now, however, and allow me to enumerate the full list of rules and conditions. Non-compliance with any one of these edicts does, of course, preclude us from even considering your petition." She turned toward the card rooms. All of her maids and footmen fell in behind her, as if following their general into war. "This way, if you please."

"The first and only location that sprang to mind?" Lord Sheffield murmured in Amelia's ear.

She stared back at him with wide eyes. "Was it not? You know how dreadful I am with recalling details."

He placed her fingers firmly upon his arm. "The only dreadful thing is the bald-faced lies spilling from that woman's mouth. She cannot possibly believe the *venue* is what brings hopefuls begging for vouchers. I have never once seen anything remotely edible pass through those supper rooms, and the ballroom! The floor has been ruined for years, and the curtains have got so thin as to be transparent."

"Minor concessions," she whispered back. "You were the one who wanted space to promenade, and a venue not already promised."

"I hadn't even told you that yet!"

She waved a hand to hush him.

"All entry shall be denied," Lady Jersey was saying now, "beginning promptly at eleven. That hour is good enough for the high Season, and it is good enough for your party."

Lord Sheffield stepped forward, his eyes fierce. Amelia checked his progress by not releasing his arm. They were lucky so many servants stood between them and Lady Jersey, or she might have taken umbrage at his obvious disagreement.

"Listen in silence," Amelia admonished him softly. "As you may recall, this is a fact-finding tour and nothing more. I will present my full report by dawn, and your word on the subject will be final."

His expression was skeptical, but he made no move to interrupt the countess.

"Furthermore," Lady Jersey continued, the back of her head barely visible beyond the cloud of servants surrounding her. "Proper dress must be worn if a guest is to be granted admission. I am sure your guests will be capable of comporting themselves in line with both propriety and fashion."

She strode round the corner. Her maids and footmen scrambled to keep pace.

"I don't care about fashion," Lord Sheffield murmured into Amelia's ear, "but I'm sorely disappointed whenever a lady I escort decides to comport herself with propriety."

Smiling despite herself, she cuffed him on the shoulder. "Pay attention. If Lady

Jersey believes you're not taking her rules seriously, she'll do worse than deny us the ballroom for your party."

"And what? Revoke my voucher?" He rolled his eyes heavenward. "There are a thousand more stimulating pursuits in this city, if one has the slightest imagination. I hardly cower before a gaggle of ladies who seek to dictate the style of my breeches."

"*You* might not notice if your membership was revoked," she answered tartly. "That is because you are already scandalous. Whether I agree with them or not, I have never once run afoul of the patronesses' fine regard."

"Good God." He leered at her suggestively. "I'm quite overcome with the desire to taint you with impropriety."

She dragged him forward without responding. She *couldn't* reply. Her mind flowed with wicked images of what he might do if it weren't for propriety. From the racing of her heart and her complete lack of breath, she needed to limit the time spent alone with him, or risk falling under his spell.

Having finished her speech on the card

rooms and what uses they could and could not be put to, Lady Jersey stood at the entranceway to the grand ballroom. She arched a brow.

"I trust you have not done anything so presumptuous as imagine a guest list without first consulting the names written in our book?"

"Oh no, my lady," Amelia replied quickly. "A Pembroke is never presumptuous."

The countess gave a sharp nod. She and her retinue disappeared into the ballroom, but Lord Sheffield was too convulsed with laughter to chase after Lady Jersey again.

"A Pembroke is never—" He snorted and shook his head. "I don't know who is the more presumptuous, you or the patronesses!"

Amelia gazed at him calmly. "I'm sure I cannot imagine to what you refer."

"You already have a guest list, don't you?" he said with a long-suffering sigh. "You hadn't even consulted *me* yet, but I'd wager a monkey you've had a list of names since before you even knocked on my door."

"With five volumes of notes and an annotated index, I should hope myself capable of compiling an exemplary guest list." She blinked angelically. "You, of course, shall have the final say."

"I shall not. Didn't you hear that woman? If the Prince Regent's name were absent from her precious book, he would be denied at the door!" Lord Sheffield's voice turned serious. "Have you truly already compiled a guest list? No, don't answer that. I know you have! I don't doubt you've got the patronesses' list memorized as well." His eyes narrowed. "How many people on mine are not on hers?"

"Forty-seven."

He stared at her, aghast. "How is that possible? *Who*?"

She shot a quick glance at the empty corridor. They ought to catch up with Lady Jersey before she noted their absence. But it was better to have this conversation without the countess in earshot. Amelia laid her hand on his arm. "Virtually all of your cousins failed to make the cut. Rarely does anyone from the countryside succeed in procuring a voucher. As for your town acquaintances, a few that held vouchers in the past have had them revoked."

His gaze darkened. "For example?"

"Captain Grey comes to mind. As does his friend, Major Blackpool."

Lord Sheffield jerked back in shock. "But they are war heroes! What can those dragons possibly have against Captain Grey?"

She touched her fingers to his arm. "If it makes you feel better, my intelligence is that he hasn't spoken a word since returning from Belgium, so I doubt he would accept an invitation regardless."

"It does not make me feel better." His muscles were rigid beneath her palm. "What about Major Blackpool? When I saw him last month, he was as clever and witty as ever."

She bit her lip. "His membership was canceled due to his refusal to comply with the dress code. Something about silk stockings being incompatible with his prosthesis."

"The man lost his leg in battle!"

"Which means he shan't wear appropriate stockings, shall he?" She gestured at the shabby opulence around them. "Rules are rules, my lord."

"Lady Jersey can take her rules and—"

The countess swept back into the room. Her pursed lips indicated she was vexed by not having been granted their undivided attention.

"Discourse," she said sharply. "Those of your guests who are not dancing—and even those who are—must comply with strict adherence to the mandates governing appropriate topics of conversation. No politics. No salacious gossip. No Corn Law riots. And absolutely no talk of war." She fixed Lord Sheffield with a speaking gaze.

He swung his eyes back to Amelia and spoke without bothering to dissimulate. "I not only cannot invite family members and military heroes who are not on the patronesses' exalted list, I'm not even permitted to verbally acknowledge the realities of war at my own party?"

"'Tisn't just your party," the countess shot back. "It is also an Almack's affair."

"It is obviously not going to be *that*," he replied flatly.

Lady Jersey lifted her chin. "Are you

trying to provoke my displeasure, Lord Sheffield?"

"With mere words? If I wished to ensure your displeasure, I should do something like *this*." He swung Amelia round and towed her toward the exit without so much as a backward glance. "Come along, darling. I believe this tour is over."

"Come *along*?" She tried to yank free of his iron grip. "Did you just give *Lady Jersey* the cut direct?"

"We both did!" he agreed cheerfully. "She's likely tearing our names from her book at this very moment. I do hope you weren't terribly attached to submitting to their gothic rules. I believe we've finally run afoul of the patronesses' kind regard."

CHAPTER 5

The next morning, Amelia did not waste her time sending Lord Sheffield a report on the benefits and conveniences of Almack's. In fact, she did not write him at all.

Although she was unquestionably out of favor with Lady Jersey at the moment, the countess was not known to hold grudges, and Amelia had every faith that their unexceptional past history—and Lord Sheffield's outspoken role in yesterday's dustup—would soon mend the ladies' broken fences. Everything was going according to plan.

Lord Sheffield sent his first missive at ten in the morning. His second missive arrived at two in the afternoon. Amelia ignored them both. At six o'clock, she tied on her prettiest bonnet and breezed out the front door just as a coach-and-four bearing the viscount's crest pulled onto the circular drive.

She smiled. He was right on time.

He leapt from his carriage just as she approached the door. "What do you mean by not responding to my missives? I sent a man with the first one to wait for a response, and had to send another just to fetch him home!" He grabbed her by the hands. "Are you cross with me? I won't allow the Jersey woman to take my ill behavior out on you. I even sent a flowery letter full of every lie I could think of to restore her good temper but I swear to you, Lady Amelia—" He straightened his shoulders. "Even if my plea for forgiveness succeeds, I will not have a Christmastide ball constrained to those edicts."

"Of course not," she said soothingly, then tilted her head toward his open carriage door. "Help me up?"

He swung her up and into the coach without pausing to ask why. Amelia found the ensuing consternation upon his handsome visage to be quite comical, though she strove to keep her amusement hidden from her face.

Lord Sheffield stared up at her from the icy drive as if he couldn't quite credit how or why they had switched places. He shook his head and hefted himself back into the carriage. "Are we going somewhere?"

This time, he seated himself beside her rather than across from her. Her heartbeat quickened. He took up far too much space. The presence of his body snug against hers heated her flesh far more efficiently than any warming brick might have done.

"Vauxhall," she answered, without demanding he switch seats. After all, it was his carriage. And a Pembroke was never presumptuous.

His bright hazel eyes widened in surprise. "The pleasure gardens? Aren't they closed for the winter?"

"They do not have to be," she told him. "Like Almack's, Vauxhall Gardens is a favorite spot for entertainment. Unlike Almack's, there are few rules governing admittance. Your entire guest list would be welcome."

His lip curled. "Further unlike Almack's, people visit pleasure gardens for *fun*."

"You don't have fun at Almack's?" she asked, too innocently.

"Tisn't called the Marriage Mart because it's conducive to bachelorhood." His brow furrowed. "Speaking of which, why haven't *you* got leg-shackled? You've got beauty, brains, elegance, and—as you previously mentioned—aren't hurting for coin. I cannot credit that a woman with your wit, looks, and politesse should have any trouble at all collecting suitors."

"'Tis my personality," she sighed, affecting a morose expression. "I cannot conceive why my beaux object to my running every aspect of their lives."

"Myopic pups, indeed." The corners of his mouth quirked. "Have you considered—between now and any future leg-shackling, that is—the possibility of spending some time *not* running things?"

"Oh, I do," she said earnestly. "Twice daily! I try very hard not to run things in my sleep, nor whilst cleaning my teeth. Far too difficult to bark orders with tooth powder in one's mouth."

He nodded gravely. "You are as wise as you are practical, Lady Amelia."

She nodded back. "I know."

But he had taken his own advice, not hers. She cut him another glance. He had broken from his schedule. It was half six on a cold but clear Thursday evening. She could not have planned it any better. "It isn't yet eight of the clock. Shouldn't you be at your desk, my lord?"

He raised his brow. "I would be, if a certain managing chit had but deigned to respond to my missives."

"Even could I swallow the absurd conclusion that only calling upon me in person would do, it doesn't explain what you're doing in a carriage with me in mid-afternoon."

His gaze softened, his voice low and warm. "Where else would I wish to be?"

She blushed and averted her face toward the window. She'd expected him to appear, *counted* on it in fact, but she hadn't imagined—had never once thought—

Perhaps he was right. Perhaps there *was* some value to setting one's duties aside now and then for a few stolen moments.

With the right person.

They alighted from the coach just before the Vauxhall Bridge. He tucked her hand in the crook of his arm and matched his steps to hers. The wind was sharp and icy as it flew across the Thames and into their scrunched faces. Lord Sheffield put himself between the wind and Amelia, sheltering her as much as possible until they had crossed to the other side.

Leafless trees provided welcome relief from the direct onslaught of the wind, but he did not release her from his side. They strolled down the paths hip-to-hip, shoulder-to-shoulder. Shoulder-to-upper-arm, to be precise. She swallowed. Her throat was unaccountably dry. He was more than half a head taller, and much larger. The difference in their sizes did not make her feel small, but rather, safe. She liked the feel of his warm strong body so close to hers, the way he huddled closer if he detected the slightest shiver.

Without candles in the lanterns, the "illuminated" walks were as shadowy as the Dark Paths. And without the ten or fifteen thousand people who crowded the walkways during the summer, it was as if the two of them strolled through their own private gardens. She held his arm a little tighter.

They might have walked for miles, so little did she notice the passage of time. She was too focused on the simple joys of their synchronized steps, the white puffs of vapor as they breathed, the smiling looks they exchanged at this statue or that tower.

The supper rooms were empty, the orchestra vacant, but rather than lend a desolate air, the grounds seemed all the more magical. Dismal for a party, of course—her toes were freezing and her lips so chapped she barely dared to speak—but she was arm-in-arm with Viscount Sheffield. There were no patrons to contend with, no patronesses to bow and scrape to, no one at all save the two of them. The winding trail their only guide, a smattering of stars their only chaperone.

Her hands went clammy. She swallowed hard. They were truly alone. Errands in the city proper were one thing, with grooms and footmen at every turn. But here...in Vauxhall...all alone beneath the stars...

He pulled her into his arms.

She *meant* to resist, or at least she probably meant to, but all she could do was gaze up at him without a word. Her blood quickened.

"We should go," he said gruffly, his face inscrutable.

"Why?" Her heartbeat thundered. She gripped his arms tight to keep herself from twining her own about his neck.

He lowered his mouth to her ear, brushing it with a feather-soft kiss. "It isn't safe."

Her answering shiver had nothing to do with the cold. She couldn't even feel the weather. Her thighs were flush with his, her breasts against his chest. She had never stood so close to any man, had never fought the urge to press herself even closer.

"What could happen?" she whispered.

He cupped her face in his hands. "*Anything.*"

Her breath caught at the ragged edge to his voice. At the delicious knowledge that it was *she* whom he desired, she who caused the tremble in his touch and the glint of hunger in his eyes.

But her life hung together on planning, not passion. She was much too sensible to allow the wants of her heart to outweigh the wisdom of her brain.

When he lowered his face toward hers, she pulled from his embrace and walked away.

CHAPTER 6

Benedict passed a sleepless night. The fact of a sleepless night was not so very wonderful, but rather the reason that kept him from his slumber.

Lady Amelia.

Because of her, he had twice broken from his schedule since the last daybreak. He'd started by leaving his office before eight the night before, simply because he couldn't stand the suspense any longer of why the woman who had insisted upon a maximum three hour turnabout for her own missives was refusing to answer his own. And then, after the lovely, charming, romantic, disappointing outing in Vauxhall...

He had returned home. He! Had returned *home.*

What did he care for gentlemen's clubs and boxing matches when all he could think about was the soft, stolen kiss she hadn't let him take? If only he hadn't warned her of his intentions...But no, he could never treat her dishonorably. Had never treated anyone dishonorably. It was the reason why he selected his mistresses from actresses and courtesans who expected nothing more than a casual physical affair.

And of course he couldn't take Lady Amelia as his mistress. Now that he'd met her, he couldn't take *anyone* as his mistress, or anything else. They all paled next to her. The debutantes were too shallow, the demimonde too world-weary, the bluestockings too desperate to prove they didn't need a man.

Lady Amelia didn't have to prove such a thing. She'd shown him with every word, every action, from the moment of their first meeting. She didn't need him, or likely anyone. But, oh, if he could make her *want* him...

The first thing she had wanted was to realize his Christmastide ball, so he supposed he ought to start there. She hadn't sent him a report this morning, but of course it hadn't been necessary. By the time they'd stepped foot on the frozen bridge, he'd finally determined what she was about.

Each location she'd presented to him had been ostensibly what he wanted. Fashionable and unimpeachable. She'd orchestrated tours of perfectly acceptable venues that he would be progressively more likely to abhor. He would never disrupt the holiday plans of others, simply because as viscount, it could be done. Nor could he condone a location—no matter how grand! —that would force him to snub his own friends and family, just to dance within its hallowed walls.

And it went without saying that pleasure gardens wouldn't do. Not in winter. The slippery paths, the leafless trees, the high likelihood of guests becoming ill or compromised or losing their extremities to frostbite...No, there was only one logical, convenient place to temporarily relocate the Christmastide ball without sacrificing any of its customs or inconveniencing any number of people.

Lady Amelia was going to get her wish of Ravenwood House after all.

Benedict scooped up his hat and shrugged into his greatcoat. He had tried as valiantly as he could to spend the scheduled twelve hours before his desk, but here it was three in the afternoon and he was on his way across Hyde Park to let her know she had won.

Not that he was breaking his schedule. He smiled. The lady was now his business.

When he arrived at the ducal estate, he was half-surprised to find the butler, not Lady Amelia, at the door. He smiled. It was high time he surprise *her* for a change.

He relinquished his hat and coat and followed the butler. Instead of ushering him to a sitting room, the butler strode to the wide, curved stairway leading to the Ravenwood ballroom. He threw open the doors without hesitation and motioned Benedict inside.

The ballroom had been transformed into a mirror of his own.

An army of servants lined the walls with gold paper. Kissing balls of bright green holly hung from various chandeliers. There was even a small sprig attached to the archway under which he stood. The dance floor was sparkling and freshly lymewashed. The table linens had all been embroidered with the Sheffield family crest.

Laughter bubbled deep inside his throat. Lady Amelia would not be remotely surprised to learn he'd come about to her way of thinking. She'd known it would happen even before they had met!

He spun about at the sound of her voice approaching from behind him. A clump of holly dangled overhead. *Perfect.* He was standing right beneath a kissing ball. He grinned. He would've kissed her even if he wasn't. The moment she came into sight, he swung her into his arms and covered her mouth with his. She yielded to his embrace as if she, too, had spent a sleepless night yearning for his kisses, for his touch. He held her tight. She was maddening and managing and by God was he going to make her his.

Her lips were warm, her mouth hot. She tasted like honey and peppermint. Her hair was soft beneath his fingers. He pulled her closer. His body was hard, every pore aflame. He had dreamt of this moment since he first met her. Had dreamt of her hair tangled in his fingers, her curves pressed flush against him. Now that he had her, he had no wish to ever let her go.

When he finally released her from his arms, he discovered a pair of bright green eyes staring at him from over Lady Amelia's shoulder. Pembroke eyes. Lady Amelia had not been in conversation with one of the many servants assigned to the ball, as Benedict had presumed, but rather with her brother. The Duke of Ravenwood. Bearing clusters of holly in his arms. Waiting for them to finish kissing so he could manage the stairs without needing to step around them.

Benedict coughed into his hand, then gestured weakly toward the kissing ball overhead.

Lady Amelia's cheeks flushed scarlet.

The duke didn't even change expression. He simply continued walking.

"Sheffield," was his perfunctory greeting as he passed Benedict, but to his sister Ravenwood muttered a barely audible, "I might've known."

She turned wide eyes to her brother. "I never once thought—"

"You've never not thought in your life," he returned without pausing. "If you're at all surprised, then you've only gammoned yourself."

Benedict hauled her to his side and gestured at the bedecked walls. "At what point were you going to mention that the party decisions had already been made for me, Ravenwood?"

At this, the duke stopped mid-step and nearly choked with laughter. "Beg your pardon, Sheffield." He cast a speaking glance at his sister then turned his merry gaze back to Benedict. "Did you try to get *your* way?"

Benedict lifted a shoulder with a self-deprecating smile.

The duke clapped him on the shoulder, unabashed. "You'll learn soon enough."

Benedict gazed down at Lady Amelia. "I believe I already have."

CHAPTER 7

One week. An entire wasted week.

Benedict drummed his fingers atop his accounts ledger. He wasn't certain which circumstance was the most surprising: seven days passing since he'd last seen Lady Amelia, or the woman's absence driving him battier than her presence. She had allowed that single, stolen kiss beneath the holly—and ignored him ever since. He ground his teeth.

Something had to be done.

One might suppose he could simply wait two more days until the evening of his Christmas Eve ball, but no. Benedict could not. He had *tried*.

It was four o'clock on Friday afternoon and the only thing he'd accomplished in the past seven days was wondering what Lady Amelia was doing—and vainly trying to convince her to spare him a bit of her time. He rubbed his temples. When he'd short-sightedly given her carte blanche on the decorations, he'd inadvertently spoiled the sole reason she'd had to contact him. And so she had not.

Benedict had jotted missives and left calling-cards and sent a wagonload of flowers...to no response. Lady Amelia was not other people. Or even most people. She was unique and fetching and too bloody efficient to pen unnecessary notes to hopelessly smitten viscounts who wished to waste her time eating ices at Gunter's or visiting the Egyptian Hall in Piccadilly.

Merely wishing for her company was not reason enough for her to grant it. He sighed. The silver lining to her strict adherence to efficiency was that the sole solution couldn't have been clearer: He would simply have to invent some pretext wherein he didn't just *want* her. He *needed* her.

And then he'd whisk her somewhere else entirely. Somewhere less tepid than lemon ices and Egyptian relics. She could do those things with anyone of her acquaintance, any time she wished. If he intended to prove that time spent with him was not only an experience worth having, but one she could not have with anyone else—well, he would have to make certain that happened. The sort of evening only a reformed rake could offer.

But first, he had to lure her from her efficient cage.

He selected a fresh sheet of parchment and sighed heavily. Nothing for it. He was forced to tempt her with the one thing she won't be able to resist: the opportunity to lend her quick, clever brain toward the management of his estate. He dipped his pen in the ink and marveled at the steadiness of his fingers.

A fortnight ago he had balked at the idea of accepting help with a party he had no time to arrange. And now, he was prepared to offer much more than that. He would invite her to share everything. If she would only accept the invitation.

He smiled. She was not the only one capable of maneuvering others to do her will.

My dearest Lady Amelia,

I find myself in the position of requiring an independent perspective on a small matter pertaining to resource allocation, and my head steward shan't return until after Christmastide. If you would be so kind as to lend your practical brain to the affair, the problem could be resolved this very day.

That said, do come at once or not at all—I depart for Grosvenor Square at the stroke of eight. I've extremely impractical plans for a loud, bosky evening, and you know how loathe I am to break from schedule.

Yours Etc,

Benedict Sheffield

There. He signed with a flourish and grinned at the scrawled words. 'Twas the perfect mix of annoying and tempting. Either way, Lady Amelia would be unable to resist giving him a piece of her mind. In person. Tonight.

He franked the missive and instructed his footman to await a reply. In the meantime, he summoned his servants into the main parlor for a brief conference.

"Soon, you are to expect the arrival of Lady Amelia Pembroke. Some of you might remember her as the young lady who'd brought a book to read and rugs to sit upon in full expectation of being forced to wait to be granted an appearance. From this moment onward, she is to be granted immediate access to anything she desires including, but not limited to, my company."

His butler's face blanched at the thought of accepting a guest without prior appointment. "Immediate access...After eight o'clock?"

"Immediate access immediately. Regardless of the hour." Benedict turned from Coombs to address the rest of his staff. "Now then. Lady Amelia believes she has been invited to offer suggestions regarding certain resource misallocations in the household."

"*What* resource misallocations?" his housekeeper demanded hotly. Mrs. Harris had managed the underservants since before Benedict had inherited the viscountcy and prided herself on knowing every inch of the estate.

He waved a hand. "I've no idea, but I cannot overstate the importance of allowing Lady Amelia to offer insightful suggestions."

Coombs cleared his throat. "We're to...humor the lady?"

"Humor her?" Benedict paused. There once was a time when he too thought such a feat was possible. This was no longer a meaningless game—if it ever had been.

The only prize worth winning was her heart. She was already in possession of his. "No. Please treat her as if she will become your future mistress. With luck, I can make that happen."

CHAPTER 8

Amelia clasped her hands behind her back and forced herself not to frown. She, who prided herself on always knowing everything, was unaccountably...suspicious.

Lord Sheffield's servants were forthcoming and respectful, and the viscount himself had neither abandoned her to her fate, nor was he looming over her shoulder. And yet she couldn't shake the sensation that she was being evaluated very closely. Not only by him, but by his entire staff.

The last time she'd called upon the Sheffield town house, she'd been nothing more than a curiosity. Now the servants stared at her *with* curiosity. Not one had taken their eyes from her as she interviewed this footman or that scullery maid, no matter how mundane the questions she posed. She wasn't naive enough to believe Lord Sheffield was so impressed with her ability to plan a party that he now wished for her to plan his entire life. For one thing, the party hadn't happened yet. She couldn't expect miracles until she'd fully proven herself. Perhaps after Sunday...

"Thank you, John." She inclined her head to dismiss the coachman and turned toward Lord Sheffield's butler. "Coombs, if I may have a moment of your time?"

The butler's eyes widened at her use of his name.

She kept her expression bland, as if she had not spent the entire carriage ride frantically flipping through all five journals to commit to memory the names and descriptions she'd managed to capture over the years. It was by no means an exhaustive list —she'd had no occasion to come in contact with his lordship's laundry maids or private valet—but she had a fine start on a goodly number of footmen, grooms, and other individuals. The names she learned today, she carefully committed to a new shelf in her memory pantry.

Desserts. Because Lord Sheffield was delicious.

She forced herself to focus on the task at hand: commit every detail of the Sheffield household to memory and then prove herself invaluable to the household's future. It had become painfully clear that the only future she wanted was one with Lord Sheffield. Had she honestly thought only a duke or earl would do? That selecting a husband was no more complicated than choosing an appropriate name from a worn copy of *Debrett's Peerage?*

A husband was so much more than a title and a lineage. A husband was an invigorating, infuriating, intoxicating whirlwind of wit and passion and adventure. She could not imagine spending the rest of her life with anyone but Lord Sheffield. To do that, she needed to show him and his staff that they needed her, too.

Lord Sheffield stepped up behind her as she concluded her interview with his butler.

She knew he was there, not because his

footsteps had betrayed any sound or his butler had so much as blinked an eye, but because her body simply *knew* when he was near. Her heartbeat doubled. Her breaths came faster—or not at all. Every inch of her skin tingled with expectation, hoping for his touch. If his town house were strewn with half as many kissing balls as currently adorned the Ravenwood ballroom, perhaps Lord Sheffield might have reprised the moment, instead of keeping a respectful distance and...glancing at his pocket watch?

She tried not to grind her teeth. "Late for your bawdy evening, I take it?"

The wicked glint in his hazel eyes sent a flash of heat to her core. "Eight o'clock. We're right on time." He helped her into her pelisse. "Now that you've met my staff, what are your recommendations?"

"My—" Her mouth fell open as she stared at him in shock. "I cannot give recommendations without proper analysis. I have spent the past two hours interviewing dozens of individuals and cannot possibly begin to speculate on reorganizing tasks and schedules until I've had a chance to transcribe the information they've shared with me and check each servant's duties and understanding against—"

He placed her hand on the crook of his arm and spun her toward the door. "When do you think you'll have that ready? Tonight's already spoken for in my case, but if you send a report round first thing tomorrow, I shall have a look at it with my morning tea." He pushed open the door. "First thing meaning eight o'clock, of course. I intend to return home very late, and possibly very drunkenly. It all depends on how the evening goes."

So much fire licked through her veins at the thought of how he intended to spend his evening that she didn't feel the bitter wind against her bare cheeks or the flakes of snow upon her eyelashes. "That's very nice! I should be at my desk calculating time analyses and drawing schedules while you are up to your cravat in devilry. The exact sort of evening I was hoping for."

"Were you? Then you were the right person to call, because there's nothing I find more tedious than time analyses. Except Lady Jersey. And musicales." As he handed her into the carriage, his tone turned contemplative. "Although I suppose it could be argued that I get up to as much devilry there as anywhere. How about you, Lady Amelia?" He plopped down on the squab next to her. "When was the last time you were up to your fichu in mischief?"

"I have never in my life been up to devilry *or* mischief, because I am far too practical to fritter my valuable time on the sort of nonsense you—"

"Lean forward." Something feathered and black fluttered before her eyes.

She jerked her head back. "What in the—"

"I said forward, not backward." He cupped the base of her head with his hand as the feathery object returned to her face. Peacock feathers. Papier-mâché. Eye holes. *A mask.*

A mask?

She stared at him through the almond-shaped cutouts as he fastened the ribbon about her head. "I have no idea—"

"Of course you don't," he said smugly. "'Twould have been a poor surprise indeed if you'd had an idea."

"I'm never surprised," she grumbled.

"You bundled me into my pelisse and then up into your carriage—obviously we were going somewhere. But a *masquerade*?"

"I thought you were never surprised."

She lifted her chin and glared at him. "If you had but asked, I would've informed you that I do not attend masquerades."

"That is precisely why I didn't ask." He tied a brightly colored mask behind his head and grinned at her.

She tried not to find him devastatingly handsome. "Masquerades are frivolous, scandalous—"

"Scandalous?"

"People in costume lose their minds completely. The 'ladies,' if there are any, have been known to be free with their favors and dampen their gowns to make them more transparent—"

"I did bring a bowl of water, in case you wished to blend with the masses."

She smacked him on the shoulder. "I should dump it on your head. What will people think when they see *me* at a masquerade?"

"They won't see you. That's the whole point. We won't know who *they* are, either."

"Then what use is going? If one cannot catch up with old friends or forge connections with new acquaintances—"

"Anonymity is its own reward. There's something to be said for doing whatever you like without fear of judgment. It's an experience to be sampled at least once in your life." His eyes glinted behind his mask as he lowered his mouth to her ear. "If you like this one, I can think of a few more not-to-be-missed experiences."

Gooseflesh trickled down her spine. She was saved from having to respond verbally by the carriage rolling to a stop.

Somewhat saved. Her jaw fell open in disbelief when she realized where they were. "The Duke of *Lambley's* house? Are you mad?"

"He's a duke, like your brother." Lord Sheffield leapt out of the carriage. "How can you possibly object?"

"He's nothing like my brother! His name is in the scandal sheets even more than yours. Duels in the park, wild curricle races, demimondaines at his soirées..." She groaned into her hands. "*Please* tell me we will not be under the same roof as demi-mondaines."

"That's the beauty of a masquerade—nobody knows!" He swung her out of the carriage and into his arms. "Tonight, I want you to close your memory pantry and enjoy the moment. There's no report due in the morning. Or ever. There's just you and me and an orchestra waiting for us to come and dance."

She held on tight as he whisked her from the curb to the front step. There was plenty of time to say no. To tuck herself back into the carriage and return to her safe, predictable world.

But she'd discovered over the past fortnight that dull predictability wasn't what made life enjoyable after all.

Lord Sheffield's unpredictability was part of what made him so irresistible.

He hadn't agreed to her Christmastide schemes because she'd manipulated him into it, but rather, for reasons of his own. He spent the evening with her solely because he chose to do so. Because he'd chosen *her* over the thousand-and-one other women vying for his time and his heart.

She allowed the Duke of Lambley's butler to relieve her of her pelisse, but she would not allow anyone to separate her from Lord Sheffield. She looped her hand around his arm and stood far too close for propriety. The edge of her breast was in constant contact with the hard muscles of his upper arm. Her entire body pricked with awareness.

With the feathery mask tied before her eyes, she could not cast sidelong glances in his direction. She let herself gaze up at him openly. Drink him in. The breadth of his shoulders in his sharp black coat. The fullness of his lips. Her heart thudded. She was falling hard. She bit her lip, but could not force herself to look away.

He led her straight into the ballroom, where dozens of masked couples swirled to a languid waltz. A footman approached bearing a tray of sparkling wine. Lord Sheffield motioned the footman away before he could offer them a glass of champagne.

"Forgive me," he murmured in Amelia's

ear. "I cannot wait another moment to have you in my arms."

Her legs trembled.

He swept her onto the dance floor. His steps were perfect, his gaze unshakable, his embrace scandalously tight, even for a waltz.

She let him pull her closer. She preferred the warmth of his arms over a glass of champagne any day of the week. She tried not to think about what she would do once Christmastide had come and gone.

Would he still think of her after his party concluded? She had not been able to think of anything else for two weeks. The arguments she'd given herself for why they would not suit seemed as flimsy as the lace fichu protecting her bosom. He worked as hard as he played, and now *that* was suddenly in question.

His name had been absent from the scandal sheets since the day they'd visited Vauxhall Gardens. At first, she had presumed his lack of exploits was because she had monopolized his evenings. But he'd gone out after that first night at the theatre and again after their disastrous encounter with Lady Jersey. From that moment in the pleasure gardens when he *could've* stolen a kiss, but *didn't*...There hadn't been one peep of Viscount S—'s night ventures. As far as she knew, he hadn't so much as left his town house.

Until now. Here. With her. Hope flooded her heart.

The music faded into silence and the orchestra took a small break. Although the waltz had ended, he did not release her from his arms. One by one, the other couples left the floor in search of champagne or darkened corners. Masked revelers lined the perimeter, but only she and Lord Sheffield remained on the dance floor.

All eyes were on them.

Masked, she reminded herself as her heartbeat spiked. *No one knows who we are. We could be anyone.*

Lord Sheffield tucked a stray tendril behind her ear and cupped her cheek in one hand. "Do you see a kissing ball anywhere?"

"N-no." She darted a quick glance about the room. It was decorated as a Venetian masquerade, not as a Christmastide celebration. There was no holly to be found. "Why do you ask?"

"Because I don't want you to think I have any reason for doing this other than because I wish to."

Before she could do more than part her lips in question, he slanted his mouth over hers.

His mouth was soft but firm against hers. His tongue hot and spiced of sweet tea and lemon. Masked or not, her heart raced at the idea of doing such a shocking thing, here, in front of so many witnesses.

Yet she had no wish to stop. She twined her hands about his neck and pulled him closer.

The feathers of his mask tangled with the feathers of her own, and for one rash, glorious second she considered ripping the mask from her head rather than break the kiss.

She had never had such a foolish thought in her life. Or felt so *alive* as she did with Lord Sheffield. Or wished so desperately for the night to never end.

When he lifted his mouth from hers, she felt the loss to her very soul.

CHAPTER 9

Christmas Eve. Amelia stood at the head of the stairs and surveyed the elegant crush of people swirling below. The viscount was never without a mob of well-wishers. Every face was animated, every mouth smiling. The ballroom might have been transported directly from the Sheffield estate. The kitchen had outdone itself. The orchestra had never sounded finer. The kissing balls were an unqualified success.

Yet she fought the most appalling urge to wring her white-gloved hands.

She couldn't recall the last time she'd suffered from such an unlikely sensation as *nerves*. Why should she? Not when she managed everyone and everything she ever interacted with down to the minutest detail. Tonight's gala was no exception. It was perhaps the most painstakingly orchestrated soirée of her entire career. And while she had no prior history of giving herself over to fun at such gatherings, they had never previously caused her neck to sweat and her stomach to twist...until today.

Viscount Sheffield's seventy-fifth annual Christmas Eve ball had to be *better* than perfect. *She* needed to be better than perfect.

She was doing this for him.

A voice came from behind her. "My lady? A note has just arrived for you."

She turned her back upon the whirling madness below to behold one of her footmen bearing a small silver tray with a single folded missive. Her fingers shook as she plucked it from the tray. She had absolutely no reason to fear such a small square of parchment, save for its very unexpectedness. This was not the regular post. The only exterior writing was a single word: *Urgent*.

With an incline of her head to dismiss the footman, she unfolded the missive and read the contents therein:

Boo.

SHE FROWNED. *Boo?*

Before she could call out to her footman to interrogate him on the missive's origin, two strong arms encircled her from behind. She bit back a shriek. The missive tumbled from her fingers as her captor spun her to face him. *Lord Sheffield.* Her lips parted. He covered her mouth with his, searing her. Branding her. Leaving her breathless.

"Boo," he whispered in her hair, then pointed a finger at the ball of holly overhead. "Did I surprise you?"

Growling, she pushed him on the shoulder. "You frightened the stuffing out of me!"

"So it *can* be done!" He grinned at her. "I win!"

She laughed. "Were we playing?"

"Were you not?" He swung her in circles and stole another quick kiss before setting her at a respectable distance. Perhaps semi-respectable. The twinkle in his eyes indicated he might kiss her again at any moment. "Thank *you*. The party is everything you said it would be and more than I ever dreamed." He frowned. "My sole complaint is that you're not dancing."

"I mustn't." She gestured toward the crowd. "I'm working."

"You're not working! You're standing on the stairs." He linked her arm with his. "Wouldn't dancing with me be a tiny bit more diverting?"

She leaned her head on his shoulder. "I can't oversee the staff and monitor the guests' comfort if I'm twirling about with you."

"Precisely. When was the last time you let yourself do as you wished, without analyzing or managing? Never?"

She opened her mouth to agree with him (she could no more cease analyzing than she could stop breathing) when she realized it was no longer true.

"Once," she said in wonder. She held herself perfectly still as she finally admitted the truth. The world hadn't ended just because she'd ceased managing it. She peered up at him from beneath her lashes. "At the masquerade. With you."

"Have you enjoyed your time with me?" he asked softly. The unwavering intensity in his eyes gave the impression he might be holding his breath.

She smiled up at him. "You know I have."

"Then let's dance." He pulled her back into his arms, his face serious. "Enjoy the moment with me, my love. Not just today, but every day. I want you in my arms for the rest of my life."

Her legs trembled. Once again, he'd managed to surprise her. As she twined her arms about his neck, she was struck with the sneaking suspicion that as much as she'd been guiding him into making the party decisions she'd already chosen for him, he'd been just as skillfully steering *her* down a path of his own.

"Have you maneuvered me into falling in love with you?" Her voice was teasing, but her eyes surely betrayed all the joy in her heart.

"It would be *impractical* for me to be the only one of us in love." He affected an exaggerated leer. "My next step is to maneuver you right into the marriage bed."

"And to think," she said, rising on her toes to kiss him. "I'd been planning the very same thing."

THE END

I HOPE you enjoyed this free short story!

If you liked this story, please consider leaving a review. Every review helps other readers find books they'll love!

WANT MORE LADY AMELIA?

Grab a FREE bonus epilogue:

Just click on http://ridley.vip/amelia for a FREE Lady Amelia bonus story!

WANT the next book in the series?

Keep turning for a sneak peek at *The Earl's Defiant Wallflower*!

Get it now: Grab your copy here!

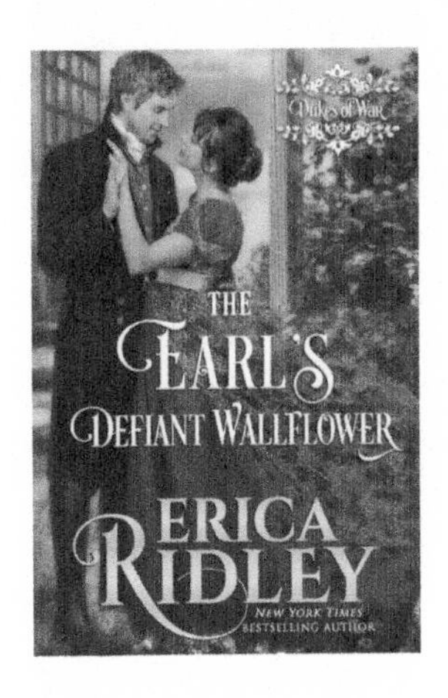

Let's hang out: "Friend" me on Facebook, Twitter, or Instagram!

Keep turning for more goodies!

THANK YOU FOR READING

Love talking books with fellow readers?

Join the ***Historical Romance Book Club*** for prizes, books, and live chats with your favorite romance authors:

Facebook.com/groups/HistRomBookClub

Check out the ***12 Dukes of Christmas*** facebook group for giveaways and exclusive content:

Facebook.com/groups/DukesOfChristmas

Join the ***Rogues to Riches*** facebook group for insider info and first looks at future books in the series:

Facebook.com/groups/RoguesToRiches

Check out the ***Dukes of War*** facebook group for giveaways and exclusive content:
Facebook.com/groups/DukesOfWar

And check out the official website for sneak peeks and more:
www.EricaRidley.com/books

THE EARL'S DEFIANT WALLFLOWER

Oliver York returns from war to find his father dead, his finances in arrears, and himself the new Earl of Carlisle. If he doesn't marry an heiress—and fast!—he and his tenants are going to be pitching tents down by the Thames. He definitely shouldn't be trading kisses with a penniless debutante...no matter how captivating she is!

Miss Grace Halton is in England just long enough to satisfy the terms of her dowry. But a marriage of convenience isn't as easy as she'd hoped. Back in America, her ailing mother needs medicine only Grace's dowry can afford. Which means the dashing earl she can't get out of her mind is the one man she can't let into her heart.

Get yours now!

SNEAK PEEK

THE EARL'S DEFIANT WALLFLOWER

January 1816
London, England

It could be worse, Lord Carlisle reminded himself as he trained his narrowed eyes on this newest battlefield. It had been three years since he'd set foot in a ballroom. The styles had changed and the faces had aged, but London soirées were as treacherous as ever. He tried to relax. At least no one was shooting at him.

When he'd left home, he'd been plain Mr. Oliver York, heir apparent to a silent dictator whom he'd been certain would live forever. Full of ennui and patriotism, he'd defied his father and skipped off to fight the French with his three best friends. Because what was the worst that could happen?

Answer: War.

He'd lost all three of his best friends. Edmund had been felled by an enemy rifle. Xavier hadn't spoken a word in months. And Bartholomew… Oliver had lost that friend when he'd had the bad grace to save the man's life.

Not that Oliver could blame him. Bart had made it back to England without his left leg or his brother. He would rather have died than let go of his dying twin. He would have succeeded in that endeavor, had Oliver not hefted his mangled body in his arms and speared his way through the bloody battlefield to the last surviving sawbones.

It was a miracle the man survived. An even bigger miracle that he hadn't picked up the first blade he'd chanced upon and driven it between Oliver's ribs.

Heroes, all of them. Heroes and murderers.

They each had blood on their hands.

Scars in their hearts. One couldn't slice a bayonet through someone else's neck to save one's own, and then pick right back up in London with carriage races and drunken wagers.

Drunken, yes. He was very good at drunken. Alcohol was the only thing that dulled the anger. And the guilt.

There had been no postal service on the front lines, so he'd actually made it all the way to his front door before the rest of the news had reached him.

He'd lost his father. Oliver was earl now. *Congratulations.*

His father—per the subsequent scandal sheets—had come to his untimely end in the bed of his latest mistress, when her cook, unaware of his seafood allergy, had sent a tray of salad tossed with lime and prawn to the lovers' boudoir.

Death by salad. And just like that, Oliver inherited an earldom.

He didn't know a button about being earl, of course. His father had rarely even spoken to him; therefore Oliver was in no position to replace him. It would take months just to go through the journals and correspondence. Let alone set about producing an heir.

Nor was he in the market for a wife. He could scarcely be responsible for one. He was having a hard enough time wrangling this beast of an earldom without adding a dependent to the mix. Not with his future uncertain, his past a nightmare.

Men of his class didn't marry for love. Men with his past shouldn't marry at all.

War had taught him that there was no vulnerability like being helpless to save someone he cared about. Like his best friends.

Xavier still had a chance to recover. At the moment, he was propped up in the library like a great silent doll, but Oliver had faith his listless friend would come out of his fugue.

That belief was precisely why Oliver, savior of all people who did not wish to be saved, had shoved his friend into a carriage and forced them both into an environment alive with lights and color. He might be dead inside, but he refused to allow the same to happen to Xavier.

Captain Xavier Grey had once been the jolliest rattle of them all. Now, he was one ragged breath away from catatonia.

Surgeons were at a loss. He was more dead than alive, but there was nothing visibly wrong with him. Perhaps all he needed was some re-assimilation. Wine. Women. Dancing. A reminder of what they'd fought for, and what was still worth living for.

So Oliver had sent for his friend and an army of tailors. The two of them could out-dandy Brummel himself. Xavier had been easy enough to shepherd along, since he was mute and pliant as waxwork. Perhaps a smidgen more lifeless.

And now they were at a ball. One look at Oliver's face ensured no one would deny them entrance. But what was he to do with Xavier? He had fallen off his chair when Oliver had attempted to seat him in the ballroom with the spinsters, so Oliver had been forced to settle him in the library, in a wingback chair with plenty of pillows.

That had worked. Somewhat. The man hadn't changed position in the past two hours, and would likely sit there like a lump of clay right through Armageddon.

Oliver trudged from the library back to the ballroom. He clearly wasn't curing Xavier tonight. Maybe the one most in need of wine, women, and dancing was Oliver himself.

Except the ratafia was warm, the wine bitter, the music off-pace. The debutantes were only attracted to his ignominiously gained title. The men only approached him to hear gore-splattered war stories Oliver had no inclination to retell, much less relive.

Ballroom Waterloo. The deafening orchestra, the cloying perfume, the swirls of satin and lace—it was as much a hell as the battlefield he'd escaped.

Anybody who fantasized about war was an imbecile. Anyone who fantasized about inheriting a title was an even bigger imbecile. This whole ballroom was chock full of imbeciles, and Oliver was the biggest of them all for thinking Xavier was a soldier he could save, this soirée a skirmish he could win. He didn't know these people anymore. He wasn't certain he even wished to. He curled his hands into fists.

Look at them planning their attacks. Sharpening their rapier wits. All of them, pawns in the same war, playing the parts they were born to play. He could no more have escaped inheriting his earldom than a wallflower could avoid being labeled a—

Oliver frowned. Brow furrowed, he squinted through the swirl of dancing couples and frowned again.

There was a girl. Across the room. Pressed into the wallpaper. A pretty girl who didn't know her part.

Not a wallflower, this young woman, despite her back-to-the-wall stance. True wallflowers dressed in drab colors and did their best to blend with the shadows. This one wore a gown with enough silk and lace to befit an empress. The colors could blind a peacock. Her cleavage would tempt the Prince of Wales himself.

And yet, something about her gave the impression that her come-hither bodice and opulent trappings were nothing more than costuming. The true her—whoever that might be—was hidden from the naked eye. Oliver tilted his head. Something in the set of her jaw, the stiffness in her spine, the softness of those ripe, full lips...

Even as he watched, she trapped her plump lower lip beneath a row of straight white teeth. Dark hair. Pale skin. Voluptuous curves. He shifted his weight.

This Snow White belonged to a different type of bedtime story. What man wouldn't want those soft red lips on every part of his body? She must've infatuated half of London by now. The delicate lace at her bosom, the way those thick black lashes blinked a few more times than strictly necessary...

Oliver's intrigued half-smile died on his face as he realized the truth. This wasn't coquetry. His enticing wallflower was uncomfortable. Nervous. His jaw tightened. Where the devil was her chaperone? Her friends? Hell, her suitors? She was utterly alone. Someone this beautiful, with skin that fair and hair that dark couldn't have any difficulty attracting a man.

"Got your eye on the new one, Carlisle?" came a sly whisper from behind Oliver's shoulder. "Better dip your wick now, before all the others have their way.

Miss Macaroni won't be looking half as nubile once she's had a mouthful of—"

"Macaroni?" Oliver interrupted, barely managing to tamp down his impulse to plug his fist into the speaker's face, sight unseen. He wouldn't be able to resist the temptation for long. War did that to a man.

The voice chuckled. "Eh, she's a Yank. Best thing for anyone to do is keep a hand over her mouth, because you can't understand a single word coming out of it."

Oh, mother-loving shite. That was Phineas Mapleton talking. The *ton*'s worst gossip.

"Not that anyone'd want her for conversation anyway," Mapleton continued. "Every female worth her salt has already given her the cut direct. The only creatures putting themselves in her path now are the desperate hostesses and the profligates planning to give her a tumble or two. Dirty money, dirty gel. Not much else a chit like that can hope for. Old man Jarvis already put his name down in White's as being the first to tup her. Got fifty quid on it, myself. Want to add your name to the pot?"

Oliver's lip curled in disgust. Ballrooms

were treacherous indeed. This jackanapes had an innocent American in his sights. One who didn't even seem to have a duenna, much less friends to keep away wolves like Mapleton.

His temples began to throb as he forced his fists to unclench. This was a different type of combat, he reminded himself. The worst thing to do would be to make a scene with Mapleton. The scandal would be horrific.

Yet he couldn't walk away. Not when the wallflower needed *rescuing*. His goddamn Achilles' heel, no matter how disastrous the outcome tended to be. He wished his heroics would work out for once.

He kept his eyes trained on the pretty black-haired American, every muscle tensed for action. An eternity ticked by. No one approached her. She had no one to dance with, to talk to. She looked… lost. Hauntingly lonely. Frightened and defiant all at the same time.

'Twould be better for them both if he turned around right now. Never met her eye. Never exchanged a single word. Left her to her fate and him to his.

It was already too late.

Want to keep reading?

Download it now!

ONCE UPON A DUKE

Beware romantic spirits from Christmas past...

Due to the terms of an estranged relative's will, the Duke of Silkridge must revisit the cold, unforgiving mountains where he lost everything he once loved. As soon as he restores his family legacy, he'll return to London where he belongs. He definitely won't rekindle the forbidden spark crackling between him and the irresistible spitfire he'd left behind...

Noelle Pratchett is immune to charming scoundrels like the arrogant duke. He stole her heart, stole a kiss, and then stole away one night never to return. Now he's back—

and they both know he won't stay. But how can she maintain her icy shields when every heated glance melts her to her core?

The *12 Dukes of Christmas* is a laugh-out-loud historical romance series of heart-warming Regency romps nestled in a picturesque snow-covered village. After all, nothing heats up a winter night quite like finding oneself in the arms of a duke!

Get Yours: Grab ***Once Upon a Duke*** here!
(Keep turning for a sneak peek!)

SNEAK PEEK

ONCE UPON A DUKE

Benjamin Ward, the fifth Duke of Silkridge, didn't want to mingle with the other guests in this godforsaken castle. He wanted a room for the night, he wanted his mother's locket, and he wanted to be gone.

Before he could have any of these things however, he caught sight of golden blond hair and laughing brown eyes. Just like that, his world tilted on its axis.

Noelle was here. *Right* here.

His heart beat uncomfortably fast.

She looked both the same and yet somehow even better than before. Soft curves and gold-rimmed spectacles. Happy and smiling and beautiful. Surrounded by a group of equally cheerful friends.

He'd thought she would be gone. He'd *hoped* she would be gone.

So many years had passed since he'd last seen her. For the longest time, he had expected her to have a Season in the capitol, to take London by storm. Perhaps she had done so, and he had missed it. After all, he spent his days in the House of Lords and his nights in his study.

Perhaps she was now "Lady" or "Mrs." and no longer the Miss Noelle Pratchett he remembered.

He didn't want details, he reminded himself. Learning she'd found someone else would serve no purpose, and discovering she was still unwed would not signify. And yet he couldn't help but gaze at her hungrily as she broke from her friends and made her way to the refreshment table, right in his direction.

The moment she caught sight of him, she pulled up short. All traces of laughter disappeared from her eyes. "Silkridge."

"Miss Pratchett," he replied, bracing himself for the inevitable correction.

It did not come.

"Five years," she said instead.

"You look lovely," he blurted out, and could have kicked himself. She did look lovely. He had not meant to notice, much less give any compliments.

She ignored it. Her lips pursed. "I thought I would never see you again."

"So did I," he admitted. He had missed her so much, those first few months.

After that, he had done his best to push her from his mind. One should not dwell upon things one could not have. Such as a rekindled romance.

Or forgiveness.

She crossed her arms beneath her bosom. "No doubt you're here for the will."

Ten o'clock on the morrow. He wouldn't be a single moment late.

"I shall be gone before you know it," he promised.

"No doubt." Her smile didn't reach her eyes. "You were last time, too."

Want more?

Grab ***Once Upon a Duke*** here!

ABOUT THE AUTHOR

Erica Ridley is a *New York Times* and *USA Today* best-selling author of historical romance novels.

In the new *12 Dukes of Christmas* series, enjoy witty, heartwarming Regency romps nestled in a picturesque snow-covered village. After all, nothing heats up a winter night quite like finding oneself in the arms of a duke!

Her two most popular series, the *Dukes of War* and *Rogues to Riches*, feature roguish peers and dashing war heroes who find love amongst the splendor and madness of Regency England.

When not reading or writing romances, Erica can be found riding camels in Africa, zip-lining through rainforests in Central America, or getting hopelessly lost in the middle of Budapest.

❄

Let's be friends! Find Erica on:

www.EricaRidley.com